D0607271

Henry and Mudge

IN THE

Family Trees

The Fifteenth Book of Their Adventures

Story by Cynthia Rylant
Pictures by Suçie Stevenson

Ready-to-Read

Simon Spotlight
New York London Toronto Sydney

For Connor Mancini—CR

For Dave, Kellie, and my pal, Pinewoods Gold Shield Diesel—SS

THE HENRY AND MUDGE BOOKS

First Aladdin Paperbacks Edition September 1998

Text copyright © 1997 by Cynthia Rylant
Illustrations copyright © 1997 by Suçie Stevenson

Simon Spotlight
An imprint of Simon & Schuster Children's Publishing Division
1230 Avenue of the Americas
New York, NY 10020

READY-TO-READ is a registered trademark of Simon & Schuster, Inc.
Also available in a Simon & Schuster Books for Young Readers hardcover edition.
The text for this book was set in 18-point Goudy.
The illustrations were rendered in pen-and-ink and watercolor.
Manufactured in the United States of America
18 20 19 17

The Library of Congress has cataloged the
Simon and Schuster Books for Young Readers hardcover edition as follows:
Rylant, Cynthia.
Henry and Mudge in the family trees : the fifteenth book of their adventures / story by
Cynthia Rylant ; pictures by Suçie Stevenson.
p.   cm.—(The Henry and Mudge books) (Ready-to-read)
"Level 2"—Cover.
Summary: Henry and his big dog Mudge attend a family reunion.
ISBN-13: 978-0-689-81179-1 (hc.)
ISBN-10: 0-689-81179-9 (hc.)
[1. Family reunions—Fiction. 2. Dogs—Fiction.] I. Stevenson, Suçie, ill. II. Title. III. Series.
IV. Series: Rylant, Cynthia. Henry and Mudge books.
PZ7.R982Hkk1   1997
[E]—dc20   96-19964
ISBN-13: 978-0-689-82317-6 (pbk.)
ISBN-10: 0-689-82317-7 (pbk.)
1211 LAK

Contents

The Invitation

One day Henry and
Henry's big dog, Mudge,
and Henry's parents
were sitting on the porch
when a letter came.

The envelope said INVITATION.

Henry loved invitations.

Mudge loved them, too,

because they usually

meant *cake*.

"Hurry, Dad, open it!"
said Henry.
Henry's father opened
the envelope.
"It's a family reunion!"
said Henry's father.
"At Cousin Annie's house."

"Yay!" shouted Henry.

He liked Cousin Annie a lot.

Mudge wagged.

He liked Annie, too.

She always wiped his

nose with hankies.

"You'll meet a lot
of new relatives, Henry,"
said Henry's mother.
"Great!" said Henry.

"And you'll hear
a lot of good stories,"
she said.
"Great!" said Henry.

"And you'll get a
million sloppy kisses,"
said Henry's father.

Henry looked at Mudge.
"*Uh-oh*," Henry said.

Sloppy Kisses

On the day of the reunion
Henry's family
drove to
Annie's house.

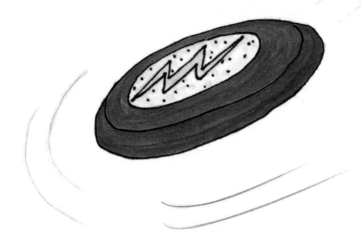

Henry brought a new Frisbee
for Annie,

a tennis ball
for Mudge,

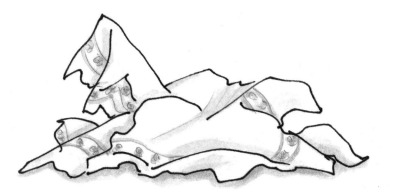

and a paper towel
for himself.
For sloppy kisses.

When they got to Annie's house,
people were everywhere.

In the yard,
on the porch,
all through the house.
And a few were even
in the trees!

Henry suddenly felt nervous.

So many relatives!

What would they say?

Would they be nice?

Would they be friendly?

Would they understand *dog drool?*

Henry and Mudge

got out of the car.

Henry felt very shy.

Suddenly Annie saw him
from up in a tree.
"Hi, Henry!" Annie called.
"Hi, Mudge!"

"MUDGE?" a relative
on a swing said.

"MUDGE?" a relative
on the porch said.

"MUDGE?" said somebody
in the house.

"Hey everybody!" shouted
Aunt Sally from another tree.
"It's MUDGE!"

And a million relatives
came running with
a million sloppy kisses—
and all of them for Mudge!
Henry smiled proudly.
Mudge wagged and wagged and wagged.

No one loved a sloppy kiss

better than Mudge.

He was made

for family reunions!

The Best Family

Henry's relatives were fun.

They danced.

They sang.

They laughed
big belly laughs.

And so many cousins!

Cousin Jeff, Cousin Joe,

Cousin Steph, Cousin Kate,

and on and on and on.

But Annie was still
the best cousin.

She and Henry and Mudge
played Frisbee with
some aunts and uncles
and grandpas and grandmas.

Aunt Sally gave Mudge
a cracker each time he
caught the Frisbee.

When they got tired,
Henry and Annie and Mudge
went to Annie's room.
Annie showed Henry
her collections of lace hankies
and china teacups.
Not very exciting,
thought Henry.

Then Annie showed
him her submarine game.
"Wow!" said Henry.
He and Annie played
submarines while Mudge
slept on the canopy bed.

Annie thought Mudge
looked cute on her
pink frilly bed.

After Mudge's nap,
they all went back
to the reunion.
They played more games
and had more fun
and climbed more trees.

Then, at the end of the day,

it was time

to say good-bye.

Henry shook a million hands
and got a million hugs.
And everyone said,
"What a fine dog you have, Henry!"
Henry was proud.
Cousins and aunts and uncles
and grandpas and grandmas
were great to have.

But Mudge would always be the
best family of all.